For Joseph and Dylan

Without whom, this story would never have been told

The Manor Tree

Rebecca Brinkman

At the edge of a field, almost hidden from view
A giant sequoia tree stood amongst smaller trees too
Children skipped on the grass with their hoops and their balls
While horses pulled heavy carts up to the Hall.

“Count up to 20!” it heard voices call out
Then footsteps as children went running about.
Playing at soldiers or jumping on benches
While their dads were away fighting hard in the trenches.

Trip-trap on the wooden bridge over the stream
Or squeezing behind it trying not to be seen.
The sequoia stood still, watching things come and go
People with dogs, kites and bubbles to blow.

It knew things of course, it had stories to tell,
Things in the village it knew only too well.
Like the fire in the church, it had heard the flames roar
And the soldiers’ parade at the end of the war.

No cars rumbled past, no planes overhead
The village was just quiet and safe, instead.

Fifty years later, a similar scene
The same redwood tree standing next to the green
In the shade of the woods with its trunk dark and wide
The Manor Tree made a marvellous spot to hide.

Another fifty years passed, people came and they went.
Sunday football, joggers and circus tents.
When the fair came to town with its rides lit up bright
Children spun on the waltzer and squealed with delight!
Manor Tree didn't just see, it *heard* things as well
Like the Thursday night ringings of St Peter's church bell.

Families young and old danced at the Gig on the Green,
The greatest live music event to be seen!
With colourful stalls, and hair full of glitter
By next morning good fairies had cleared all the litter.

WB

The May Fayre had happened year after year,

With candy floss, dog shows, acrobats without fear.

The Manor Tree took all these sights in its stride

Smiling, creating memories to treasure deep inside.

In Autumn while the other trees' leaves sailed away

Most of the Manor Tree's needles would stay.

Then during the Winter when it became colder
It saw children in scarves, each year growing older.

Two boys gazed in awe at it whenever they came
"There's The Manor Tree!" they cried…
so that's always been its name.

Now there's something amazing to tell, by the way
It's rather magic so listen carefully now, as I say:

The tree has a special gift, precious as stones
Its memories are stories, whispered into the cones!

So every redwood pine cone that lands down on the ground

Has a memory inside it that's keen to be found.

So whenever you're passing, together or alone
Carefully choose a cone, hold it and take it back home
You might paint it or spray it, silver or gold

Then hold it close to your ear for its story to be told…

Does the Manor Tree exist?

Where exactly *is* it?

read on to find out…

Quite a lot of young girls and boys probably already know the Manor Tree. Certainly, if you live in the little town of Yateley you might probably have been walking to the swings on the green.

Perhaps you play football on the green or you've taken your dog for a walk and have walked on straight past it but didn't realise!

Here are some easy steps for finding this special tree:

From the pond on the village green, turn away from the pond and start walking down the little stony path which leads East towards the village centre. You will have the large green (and, beyond that, the main road) on your left, and a smaller one on your right, through the trees.

Continue until you come to a bench on your left. Cross over the ditch which is on your right and look through the trees carefully, you'll see a small wooden bridge. Beyond this is the Village Hall. Walk over the bridge and right in front of you...

is the Manor Tree.

Photographs and illustrations: R Brinkman

Printed in Great Britain
by Amazon